NAUGHTY LITTLE PUPPY

Lisa—
Always
love
unconditionally!
☺

Sloppy Kisses!
Love,
Jellybean

B. Stiffler Smith

BEVERLY STIFFLER SMITH
Illustrated by SHANA MORROW

ISBN-13: 978-1535538732

ISBN-10: 1535538732

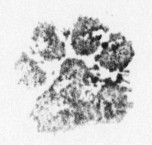

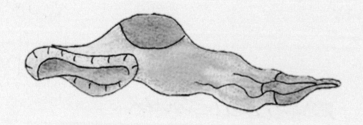

This book is dedicated to Jellybean, my silly little puppy. The unconditional love that she gives me every day has brightened my world in so many ways!

Oh no Jellybean, not my shoe!

Naughty little puppy!

Oh no Jellybean, not my sock!

Naughty little puppy!

Oh no Jellybean, not my towel!

Naughty little puppy!

Oh no Jellybean, not my toast!

Naughty little puppy!

Oh no Jellybean, not my book!

Naughty little puppy!

Oh no Jellybean, not my glove!

Naughty little puppy!

Oh yes Jellybean, my cheek!

Sweet little puppy!

I love you!

About the author.....

Now retired, Beverly spent thirty-nine years as an educator. She holds a Bachelor's Degree in Elementary Education and a Master's Degree in Educational Leadership. Beverly learned early in her career that young children are drawn to the rhythms and patterns of language often found in picture books, which has led her to fulfill her dream of becoming a children's author! Beverly's puppy, Jellybean, has been the inspiration to make this dream a reality.

About the illustrator...

Shana lives in south central Pennsylvania with her husband and son. She holds a degree in Art Education and has taught in early education and elementary schools. She is a graduate student at Penn State University and loves working with children. She greatly admires their expressive works of art and the pride they show in their accomplishments. Shana hopes that her illustrations will inspire young children to draw, color and illustrate their own stories.

About the puppy…..

Jellybean, a Shitzu/Bichon mix puppy, or Shichon, was born on a farm in Narvon, PA. Jellybean found her forever home when she was only 14 weeks old. She is now two. She loves to chase her tail and take things that do not belong to her. She makes people laugh with her silly antics. She is a certified Therapy Dog, which means she is able to visit schools, nursing homes, and community events to provide comfort and sloppy kisses to those in need. She loves making people happy!

43971082R00015

Made in the USA
Middletown, DE
07 May 2019